FINDING NELLIE

MAIL ORDER BRIDES OF FORT REGENT

SUSANNAH CALLOWAY

Tica House
Publishing

Sweet Romance that Delights and Enchants!

PERSONAL WORD FROM THE AUTHOR

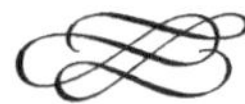

Dearest Readers,

Thank you so much for choosing one of my books. I am proud to be a part of the team of writers at Tica House Publishing who work joyfully to bring you stories of hope, faith, courage, and love. Your kind words and loving readership are deeply appreciated.

I would like to personally invite you to sign up for updates and to become part of our **Exclusive Reader Club**—it's completely Free to join! We'd love to welcome you!

Much love,

Susannah Calloway

VISIT HERE to Join our Reader's Club and to Receive Tica House Updates!

https://wesrom.subscribemenow.com/

CONTENTS

CHAPTER 1

"Eleanor Williams. How many times must I call you before you respond? Mr. Owens has been waiting for ten minutes."

The sound of her mother's voice bellowing up the stairs in their direction caused both Nellie and her younger sister Alice to break into giggles. Adelaide Williams prided herself on her gentility and good manners. It wasn't her fault her daughters so frequently provoked her to indecorous volumes.

"She sounds like a farmer calling the pigs to come and eat," Alice whispered, trying to control her laughter.

Nellie shook her head, gradually regaining her own control. "Don't be so disrespectful, Alice, you know what Mother would say if she heard you say such things."

"She wouldn't say anything," Alice said. "She'd yell it."

Nellie's giggles returned in full force, and she turned away from her sister to face the mirror once more, trying to finish the task at hand. She was well aware that Percival Owens was waiting for her downstairs – and he could continue to wait until she was finished putting her hair up in the complicated new style she'd seen so recently in the magazines from Paris. After all, there was no rush, not really.

"I don't know why you bother with that," Alice said from her seat on the bed behind her. Alice was just sixteen and had no beau yet. Nellie could remember that time in her life all too well – it had ended rather quickly, when Percy started inviting himself to dinner. Over the years, they had become friends – he was steady and reliable, as evidenced by the fact that he always showed up on time for their engagements. She, meanwhile – well, she had other things to think about.

"Percy likes it," she told her sister, pinning the last wayward brown lock into place.

"So?" said Alice pragmatically. "You don't really care what Percy likes."

"Alice. That's just downright rude – and presumptuous." She frowned at her sister in the reflection of the mirror.

"Maybe so," said Alice, shrugging, "but that doesn't mean it isn't true."

Nellie's eyes returned to her own reflection, studying it. She knew herself to be a pretty girl – perhaps one of the prettiest in their small town of Middleburg, Virginia. Percy was not the only young man to have taken notice of her, he was simply the most persistent. But he suffered from the same malady that afflicted all the men in Middleburg – they were decent, polite, upstanding, and as boring as afternoon tea with Great-Grandmother Meta. It wasn't so much that she didn't care what Percy thought, or what he liked, or anything about him at all – he had been kind and attentive to her from the very beginning, and she was not so ungracious as to think these traits without merit. But sometimes, she had to admit, she was so bored by his conversation she wanted to scream.

Was it really so wrong that she wanted something more in her life than simple, decorous boredom? The books she loved were getting her into trouble, she knew, simply because they led her thoughts down wild pathways to even wilder adventures. She wanted to experience those adventures herself – she wanted to ride a horse over a sun-baked plain, drive a runaway stagecoach to safety, be swept off her feet by a handsome cowboy and then have to nurse him back to health after some unforeseen dramatics. She did her best not to let such desires seep out into her conversation, but it was a trial at the best of times and a plague at the worst. She wanted more than anything to simply be free of the expectations that were sitting so heavily on her thin shoulders.

Her mother frowned on novels. Her father said loudly that reading was a waste of time for girls. Her future lay in marrying well and having plenty of children to carry on the Owens name and the Williams reputation. The union of the son of the richest farmer in Northwest Virginia and the daughter of the owner of the town's biggest mercantile was sure to end in peaceful, quiet happiness.

Peaceful, quiet dullness, in Nellie's opinion, which she wisely kept to herself. She'd grown up in Middleburg; she'd never been out of it in her whole life. Her only experience with the outside world was when her aunt Tilda and cousin Lacey came to visit from Richmond.

But someday, Nellie promised herself, looking herself straight in the eyes—someday, she would escape from the pleasant doldrums of Middleburg and strike out on her own, heading west, opening herself up to adventure – and to love.

In the meantime, her mother was yet again hollering up the stairs. The message had not changed, but the volume was getting steadily louder. Alice shook her head and laughed.

"One of these days, Percy's going to give up on you and go his own way," she said.

Nellie sighed and stood. Her voice was soft enough to be lost in the rustle of her skirts.

"I wish he would."

Standing up tall and squaring her shoulders, knowing she was as high-fashion as it was possible to be in Middleburg – and yet knowing too it was all a lie; she was not dressing this way for Percy but to suit her own daydreams – she left the room and started down the stairs.

Percy stood at the doorway to the sitting room, hat in hand. He gave her a smile, and the way his eyes lit up at the sight of her made her heart clench a little with regret – and guilt. She noted, as she always did, that his hair was already thinning on the top of his head, though he was only a few years older than she.

"There you are, Nell."

Down the corridor, Nellie caught a glimpse of her mother's disapproving figure, hands on her hips, before she turned and swished out of sight to leave them to their talk.

She glanced back at Percy and gave him a smile, though it was half-hearted.

"I'm so sorry to keep you waiting."

Up the stairs, she heard an undignified snort as Alice tried to restrain her derision.

"Don't give it another thought," said Percy, holding out his arm to her. "I'd wait for you to the ends of the earth."

Nellie's heart panged her even harder, the guilt rising in her chest. She liked Percy, she really did – but she did not love him, and she did not want him to love her. She wanted someone who caused her heart to beat swiftly from – well, decidedly from some emotion other than guilt. Or irritation, for that matter.

She thought of her promise to herself and wondered when she'd be able to keep it. When would her daydreams come true – and how?

But for now, Percy was waiting for her to respond, an adoring smile on his lips. She put her arm through his and managed to smile once more in return. There was nothing she could truthfully say to adequately acknowledge his devotion, and so she chose to ignore it.

"Shall we?" she said and led the way into the sitting room.

CHAPTER 2

The late summer in Fort Regent, Wyoming, brought a sheen of yellow-gold to the fields around the town that echoed the draw of the mines in the hills. As the sun began to set, late in the evening, the town was bustling: miners in town for the long Saturday, women hurrying to finish their shopping before the night encroached any further, farmers heading home with empty carts after selling their wares at the market that afternoon. Blake Irons, seated by the window in his second-story rooms over the stables, looked out on the main road through Fort Regent with a fond smile.

This was his hometown – he'd been there since he was a small child and couldn't remember anyplace else. It had its flaws, of course, but there were far more virtues. It was peaceful, quiet – even the rough ranchers, cowboys, and farmers always tipped their hats to the ladies and kept their scuffles confined to the saloon. The sheriff was actively considering taking a second job, as there seemed little call for his expertise. And in Blake's line of work, running the livery stable, the worst dust-ups that ever occurred were between horses, not humans.

He glanced down at the pen in his hand, and the sheet of paper, half-filled, that rested on the desk in front of him.

"Well, a little excitement never hurt anyone," he said aloud. "Reckon that's why I'm doing this."

He read over what he had so far.

To whom it may concern:

Dear sir or madam (He hadn't been quite sure how to start the letter)

My name is Blake Irons. I am twenty-nine years old, in good health, and reputably employed. I live in Wyoming, in a town named Fort Regent. I've decided to get married, and have been informed by a friend that writing to your establishment is the recommended method...

A small chuckle escaped him at the tense, cold language of the letter up to this point. If he didn't feel so darn awkward about the whole thing, it would certainly be easier to express himself.

"What girl's going to want a man who writes like this?" he pondered aloud, but he was still grinning at his own expense. He shook his head. "Ah well – if it's the best I can do, it's the best I can do."

There would be more than a few prayers to a benevolent Creator offered on behalf of this endeavor, and he hoped he could rely on that a little more than on his own ability to use words in a persuasive way. He did want to get married – he'd wanted to find a wife for some time now, but there just didn't seem to be anyone in Fort Regent who fit the bill. Oh, the few unmarried women who were of age were sweet and kind enough, he supposed; but though he exchanged greetings with them at church on Sundays, he had no desire to get to know them any better than that. There simply wasn't a spark, for a lack of better word – and lacking better words seemed to be a recurrent problem.

He finished the letter of inquiry, still shaking his head at himself and chuckling now and then, then folded it and slipped it into an envelope, already addressed to a well-known matrimonial agency which, according to Freddy at the post office, had offices in several large cities in the east. Freddy was the one who had told him about this in the first place, having seen a few letters come through for the same purpose. Evidently, he wasn't the only bachelor with a whim for a wife; Blake could only hope that there were enough women to go around.

He rested his hands on the sealed envelope and looked out again at the street spread beneath him. A young couple strolled by, arm in arm – Henry and Letty must have decided to make their courtship official, or her father would never have allowed her to be seen in public holding Henry's arm. Blake sent another fond smile in their direction. For the first time, he began to have real hope that he himself would find such happiness – either because of the letter he had written, or in spite of it.

CHAPTER 3

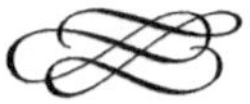

"Eleanor. Your cousin is here."

Nellie leapt up from her chair in front of the vanity, a wide smile spreading quickly across her face. She wasn't quite done with her preparations for going out, but it didn't matter – her cousin Lacey, one of her dearest friends, was far more important than what she looked like.

The feeling was mutual, as the two young women met each other halfway up the stairs. Lacey threw her arms about Nellie and hugged her tightly.

"Goodness, Nell. I thought we'd never make it this time, the train took simply *forever*."

The sound of her cousin's voice, drawn out in dramatics, made Nellie smile as it always did. Lacey lived life in a large, enthusiastic way. Coming as she did from the big city of Philadelphia, Nellie couldn't help but suspect everyone there behaved much the same. It was certainly true of Aunt Tilda, who even now was holding forth in the foyer about the deplorable lack of tea cake on the train ride over. It was a recurrent problem; on the twice-yearly visits from Tilda and her only daughter, nothing was ever quite what it was expected to be. At the bottom of the stairs, Nellie could see her mother greeting her sister-in-law with the same slightly nervous exasperation she expended on her two daughters. The sight made her grin, and she took Lacey by the hand and tugged her up the stairs in her wake.

"Come with me while I finish getting ready. We're obliged to join the Owens family for dinner."

"Obliged?" Lacey quirked an eyebrow at Nellie, then flopped down dramatically on the bed while Nellie resumed her preparations. "That's a funny word to use for an engagement with the man to whom you're practically betrothed."

"We're nothing of the sort."

"That's not what your mother told mine."

"Well," said Nellie, turning to face her reflection in the mirror. Her gray eyes were steady and resolute, she was glad to see – no trace of her upset over this was visible. "It isn't up to her, is it?"

"You could do worse…"

"It isn't a matter of doing worse, or doing better, Lacey – I simply don't love him, and I'm not about to settle down to a quiet life of doing the same thing every single day without the slightest bit of change or excitement."

Well, perhaps her emotions were showing a bit, after all. Lacey sat up and stared at her. But rather than express her surprise, she merely laughed.

"I'm willing to bet you've been wanting to say that for a very long time."

The tension in Nellie's shoulders eased a little bit, and she smiled.

"Yes, you're right – I have. But it isn't as though I can go around spouting that to everyone. My mother would have a fit. And my father…well, I'd rather not even think about it. And Alice, oh, Alice would just repeat it to everyone, thinking it was a grand joke."

"That's why I'm here," Lacey said practically. "I'm the one to say such things to – believe me, I understand. If only you could come and spend some time with me in Philadelphia, and see how things are there, outside of Middleburg…"

Nellie sighed.

"I wish I could," she said. "But you know how Father feels about that. He doesn't want me to go there without the rest of the family, and his business is far too important for him to leave for any length of time. People depend on him, you know."

Lacey caught the hint of irony in her voice and laughed again.

"I'll tell you what you should do – buy yourself a train ticket and come anyhow."

The thought brought on a vivid vision in Nellie's mind: she could just see herself, valise in hand, attired in a neat traveling suit and with a hat pinned high on her brown curls, getting onto the train. Halfway through the journey, perhaps, the train would screech to a sudden halt – bandits. The leader of the gang would come into her car, cold eyes sweeping back and forth for a likely victim. His gaze would light on her – he would be struck by her beauty, he would come to her and hold out his hand, first demanding and then simply asking that she take it…

"Nell?"

With an effort, Nellie pulled herself out of her daydream. Her cousin was smiling at her.

"What do you think? You could hop on the same train with Mother and me and come across to Pennsylvania. If we were sneaky about it, your father would never know until you were there."

Nellie sighed once more and put the finishing touches to her face powder.

"And as soon as he found out, he'd be on his way to snatch me by the collar and haul me back again, like a dog that has escaped. No, it wouldn't do any good, I wouldn't even have the chance to enjoy it." She shook her head. "Let's talk about something else. That's rather depressing."

"Hmm," said Lacey, thoughtfully. Then her face brightened. "I know what will take your mind off your troubles. A piece of juicy gossip."

"Oh, always," Nellie said enthusiastically, coming to sit beside her on the bed and drawing her feet up underneath her. It was an unladylike way to sit, but as long as her mother didn't poke her head in unexpectedly, she didn't think twice about it.

"Do you remember my friend Barbara Jinette?"

Nellie frowned thoughtfully. "I believe so – the one you always made fun of for affecting an accent?"

"Yes, that one." Lacey rolled her eyes a little. Nellie chuckled.

"It never fails to surprise me, how many friends you have that irritate you so. I suppose you joke about me, too."

"I never say anything to others that I wouldn't say directly to you," said Lacey piously. "Anyhow, you're quite different from Barbara – poor Barbara. All she's ever wanted is to be married. She'd be delighted with Percy Owens."

"She is welcome to him."

"Oh, he wouldn't have her," Lacey said, waving a hand dismissively. "Anyhow, she's no longer on the market."

"What? Barbara Jinette found a husband?"

"Found one indeed," Lacey said, grinning. "She actively went out hunting – and her prey has been cornered in Nebraska."

"Nebraska?" It sounded as foreign to Nellie as the moon. "How on earth…"

"I haven't even had a chance to tell her yet, I got the letter just before we left to come here." She opened her pocketbook and dug through it until she found an envelope, rather sadly bent and crumpled. The letter she extricated was in much the same state, but she waved it triumphantly at Nellie as though it were in pristine condition. "I read it, of course – she said I could, when it came. I think she just wanted to be sure that someone else was aware of her success."

"Start from the beginning," Nellie begged her, "this is all too confusing for me."

Taking a deep breath, Lacey did so.

"You've heard of matrimonial agencies before? Ah, of course not, I'm forgetting – Middleburg is the last place on earth to learn of new styles. Well, a matrimonial agency receives applications from unmarried women – young and old – who would like to find a husband, and then matches them up with the letters from bachelors who would like to find a wife. It's a simple proposition, really – I've even thought of starting a matrimonial agency myself, except I know my mother would have fits over it."

"Bachelors from where? Just Nebraska?"

"No – from anywhere and everywhere," Lacey said, throwing her arms wide dramatically. "Nebraska, Colorado, Nevada, Utah, all the territories – even California."

"Why don't they simply marry girls where they are? Why have them…shipped?"

"Oh, everyone has a reason," Lacey said, with the air of someone who was experienced in these things. "Perhaps they live in a tiny mining town in California, and there are few women there. Perhaps they're on the frontier and there's no women at all. And as for the girls themselves, well – Barbara Jinette is easy enough to understand. She's a sweet girl, but she has a certain…way about her. She's thrown herself at just about every marriageable young man in Philadelphia and put them all off, one by one." Lacey shook her head. "Enthusiasm is a terrible thing, unchecked."

"I see," said Nellie thoughtfully, rubbing at her chin. "Why is it that you have her letter, then?"

"Because she doesn't believe that her parents will condone her choice, of course," Lacey said frankly. "She's plenty old enough to make the decision herself, but she wanted to wait until it was a fait accompli before she told them what she had done. So her mail has been sent to my address instead. I can understand it – as challenging as Barbara is herself, her parents are even more so. A stricter set of croquet mallets I've never seen."

Lacey's uniquely casual assessment of the elder Jinettes brought the usual smile to Nellie's face, but her mind was elsewhere, whirling at a hundred miles per minute.

"Is it difficult to apply to become a bride?"

"Not at all – Barbara simply wrote them a letter of introduction and explained her situation. The agency accepted her at once; I believe they're desperate for volunteers. Evidently there are far more lonely bachelors than there are frustrated maidens."

"And how long does it take before you – before Barbara was matched?"

"The agency promises that girls will be matched within a month, but it didn't take more than two weeks before I got this letter back for Barbara." Lacey waved it at her. "This is his introduction – not quite his proposal, but I don't expect that it will take very long. And of course, Barbara won't squawk at anything he says, she'll agree immediately just to be married. She'll have to keep it under wraps just a bit longer, and then tell her parents before she leaves but after she buys her ticket."

"And they won't be able to stop her," Nellie said slowly, thoughtfully. "Because she'll already be engaged – she'll have made her decision."

"Precisely," Lacey said, nodding. "That's the beauty of it, for girls like Barbara – it isn't like courting someone locally your father disapproves of. There's no sneaking out, worrying someone will see you and tell your parents. There's only the need to rely on a good friend – someone loyal, trustworthy, and utterly beyond reproach." She laughed as she said it, jokingly, but Nellie knew full well that Lacey really did see herself this way.

In fact, Nellie saw her cousin that way, too. They'd grown up together, though so far apart, and exchanged letters regularly to keep up on the news even when they could not be together in person. Nellie had shared every wish of her heart, every daydream, every yearning for adventure with her cousin, and Lacey had never once betrayed her confidence.

She had proven herself to be trustworthy – and Nellie was ready to put her to the test once more.

"Lacey," she said, taking her cousin's hands in hers. "What would you think if I did the same as Barbara Jinette?"

Lacey raised her eyebrows at her.

"Wrote a letter?"

Nellie nodded.

"Became a Mail Order Bride?"

Another nod of confirmation. The two young women stared at each other, wide-eyed, and equally wide smiles grew slowly across their faces, mirrored in their delight.

"I think," said Lacey slowly, "you'd better find a piece of paper."

CHAPTER 4

The train pulled to a stop at last. Nellie Williams, twenty-two years of age and with her whole future stretching out in front of her like a canvas, stepped down from the platform and took a deep breath. Though the journey had been long and arduous, with many dramatic adventures, her traveling suit was as fresh and pressed as it had been the day she had left, lo these many weeks before. She cast her mind back across the expanse of the journey, dwelling with a pleasantly tingling shudder on the episode with the leader of the bandits. To think that she so narrowly avoided being abducted by that handsome man – for she could tell he was handsome even beneath the bandanna that covered his face. For a moment, her life had hung in the balance, and in the end, it was only his respect for her virtue that had conquered his desire to drag her with him back to his camp, to spend her days as the wife of an outlaw. It was a wonder, really, that her traveling suit had escaped any damage at all.

She held on tightly to her valise, which held her only belongings. So much had been taken from her, and yet she had retained the most important things: her virtue, and her ability to keep her promise to the man she'd agreed to marry.

And yet, in her deepest of hearts, she could not disavow the tinge of regret she felt when she thought of the outlaw leader and his handsome black eyes…

Now she was here, in Nebraska, ready to start her new life. She took a deep breath and stepped forward. There was a man waiting for her on the edge of the platform. He was tall and strikingly handsome. She had known he would be.

"Hello," she said calmly, extending a hand to him. "I am Eleanor Williams."

He stepped forward to meet her and took her hand in his. It was a warm, firm grip. She looked up and saw, with a leap of the heart, a pair of familiar black eyes…

"Eleanor."

She gasped. "*You.*"

"Eleanor Williams." The furious pounding on the door of her bedroom finally filtered through the layers of hazy daydream, and Nellie half-stood in a panic. Her mother's voice sounded more harassed than ever, and she was clearly fuming when Nellie opened the door.

"My goodness, girl. I've been calling you for ten minutes. What must I do to get your attention?"

Nellie gulped and shook her head.

"I'm sorry, Mother – I really wasn't ignoring you, I promise." She closed her lips tightly over the unintended addition of "…this time."

"Perhaps not, but it does seem as though you manage to mishear me – or not hear me at all – whenever the fancy strikes you." Her mother shook her head, tutting, but her irritation was ebbing as swiftly as it had arrived, as it always did. She held out the letter in her hand. Nellie recognized Lacey's writing, and her heart skipped a beat, her nerves suddenly twisting and bundling in her middle. "I only wanted to tell you the post had come, and you have a letter. Goodness, it shouldn't be so difficult to give my oldest child her mail."

"Of course, Mother," Nellie said, taking it from her, eyes raking over it greedily. Was this what she thought it might be – what she hoped it might be? It had been a whole month, and she had begun to despair of ever receiving a match from the matrimonial agency in Philadelphia. Perhaps they had decided she was unworthy of being a bride – perhaps they declined her application because she did not meet with them in person – perhaps they had tried and tried to pair her up, to no avail as bachelor after bachelor turned up his nose…

She had never been so eager to read a letter in her life. Her mother was still rambling on about her lack of attentiveness to her parents. Nellie knew her current behavior was not likely to assuage her mother's feelings about the matter, but she simply could not wait another moment.

"…and if I have to climb these stairs one more time…"

"I appreciate it, Mother, I really do. I know you have far better things to do with your time – in fact, it's nearly lunch time, and I'm sure Cook can't do without your oversight in the kitchen, considering we have guests on the way."

She ushered her mother away from the bedroom door and toward the stairs. "Yes, yes, of course I will be there at lunch. On time, too. I know Percy is coming – yes, I know he's coming to see me especially. But I really think, Mother, he's just as attached to Alice as he is to me."

She knew the words did not make much sense, but they certainly gave her mother something to think about, as Adelaide Williams quieted down and began to descend the stairs with a pensive look on her face. Nellie stifled a giggle – she'd have to apologize to poor Alice later – and fled back to her room. Closing the door firmly behind her, she threw herself across the bed and opened the letter at last.

. . .

Dear Miss Williams,

We are delighted to inform you that we have found what we believe to be the perfect match for you. Though the application process is notedly difficult when we cannot interview the applicant in person, your letter was much appreciated in its attention to detail and thorough representation of yourself, and after some deliberation it was decided that your inability to meet with our agents should not stand in the way of the fulfillment of your quest to find a suitable husband.

The gentleman in question is one Mr. Blake Irons, twenty-nine, the owner of a livery stable in Fort Regent, Wyoming. We will let his letter (please find enclosed) tell you all the pertinent details. Ideally, he would like to be married as quickly as possible, as he has already waited for some time.

Nellie couldn't help herself. She put the letters down in her lap for a moment and stared into space, then crushed them to her heart with both hands. He'd *waited for some time.* He'd been dreaming of the perfect match, just like she had – perhaps not under quite the same circumstances, but then men were different from girls, weren't they? And anyhow he lived in Wyoming – a place she knew nothing about, admittedly, but she could readily imagine it was a place full of excitement and adventure on a regular basis. No doubt he had plenty of experience with bandits and wolves and needed no such enrichment in his daydreams.

Perhaps, instead, he spent his time imagining the future to come…

A beautiful wedding, and a year later, a beautiful little boy, and a year after that a little girl, and while they whiled their lives away together, hand in hand, their happiness grew more with every single day…

She shook herself out of this daydream, which seemed to belong to someone else even though she was just as active a participant and returned to the letter. The rest of the note from the agency was filled with comments about the legality of the agreement and contingencies in case of disappointment, delay, or disapproval. She skimmed over it quickly enough to realize the agency was absolving itself of any liability for mishaps either on her journey to Wyoming, or after she arrived. Well, that was all well and good. She wasn't planning any delays; she was well equipped to deal with her parents' disapproval, and she was already certain that disappointment would not be a problem, either for herself or for this Blake Irons.

Blake Irons. His very name exuded an aura of manly strength and courage. And if he ran a livery stable, he must be very capable and hard-working. She wasn't entirely sure what running a livery stable entailed – there were none in Middleburg that she knew of, and she was relatively certain that her vague association of the job with equine-centered veterinary practice was incorrect – but that didn't matter. He was well-employed, strong, smart, and brave enough to live in a wild place like Wyoming, and most importantly of all, he had been waiting for her, Nellie Williams, to enter his life as his bride-to-be.

With her heart already bound up to this man, she opened the folded letter that accompanied the missive from the agency and began to read.

My dear Miss...

...it's strange to write to the unknown, but to know that she will be dear. I can picture you in my mind, even without having seen you. The details remain yet to be filled in, but the shape that you will occupy in my life has been waiting for you all along. It's the shape of a wife: not just a wife, but a partner, a helpmeet, a friend. I've said many a prayer over this decision, this choice to write to the agency, and by now I'm convinced that whatever happens, however the future may turn, God will grant my request.

Maybe it sounds a little crazy to say so. You might be thinking, Does he really think so much of himself? What sort of man is this – prideful, so convinced of his own self-worth. Why, he's not the sort of man I'd want to marry at all.

I'm not like that, though – really, I'm not. I'm just a fellow, plain and simple, such as you might see on any street in the world, passing by, ready to greet you with a smile and a handshake, and then understanding if you choose to move on and leave him behind. But I've never hurt anyone, and never taken advantage. My mother raised me to seek the good of others above my own, and with a clear conscience I can say I've always tried to do so – as imperfectly as I've succeeded, at times, I've always tried. I've done my best to be a good man, and I believe that goodness is rewarded. The reward that I've been asking for, searching for, is a good wife.

You'll see it isn't so much pride that moves me to write this letter – it's faith.

I can promise you, reassure you, that I am a good man and will treat you well. I work hard, but I'm not a puritan; I go to the saloon on Saturday evenings, but I'm not a drunkard. I imagine walking arm in arm with you through the town on a Sunday afternoon, introducing all and sundry to the most beautiful girl in the world, shining brightly among the others – my wife.

I reckon that life in my little town isn't going to be as easy as it might be in a big city like Philadelphia, or maybe anywhere back east. I don't suppose we have the newfangled inventions that make difficult things a little more bearable. It's a simple life, but I love it – and I hope, no, I have faith you will, too.

Waiting eagerly for your reply, standing by the door of the post office, hat in hand.

I remain yours,

Blake Irons

PS: I hope this letter isn't too crazy. After I wrote my letter of inquiry to the agency, they wrote back and said that I'd never get a girl that way. They said I should express myself, so that a girl knows what she's getting into. Well, consider yourself warned. I reckon I'm just a hopeless romantic.

Before she reached the end, Nellie could feel her eyes welling up with tears of joy. She dabbed at them with the back of her hand, sniffling. She understood exactly what he meant, saying that his faith moved him to confidence his prayer would be answered. She knew it, she felt it in her heart – wasn't her own prayer being answered, right this very moment?

"If you're willing," she said out loud – to Blake Irons or to God himself, she wasn't entirely sure, or maybe to both of them – "I'll leave as soon as you give me the sign. I'll go anywhere, even Wyoming." She frowned briefly at the letter, somewhat puzzled. "Where is Wyoming?"

Fifteen minutes later, with the atlas she'd liberated from her father's study, her curiosity was assuaged – and stoked, at the same time. It was so far away. There was so much distance to cross, so many days of travel to endure…

There was the adventure of a lifetime ahead of her.

And with a certainty like faith flaming in her heart, she knew her future was about to begin.

CHAPTER 5

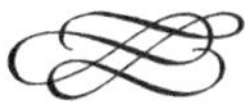

Of course, nothing happened as quickly as she would have liked.

She wrote to Blake as soon as she could, slipping out of the house to deliver the letter to the post box on the corner. It was dangerous to give her own home as the return address, rather than direct it through Lacey in Philadelphia, but she felt she could not wait any longer than she must.

It would be long enough already, she knew. The mail did not travel instantaneously; even within Middleburg, communication sometimes took two days to get from one side of the town to the other. It was usually a swifter and more reliable option to simply go round to the other's house and tell them your message in person. But as this was not possible when writing to Wyoming, Nellie made up her mind to be patient.

Oh, Lord, but it was difficult to be so.

Patience had never been one of her strong suits. And the days seemed to crawl by, followed by weeks at the pace of a sickly snail. Every day seemed the same, more monotonous than ever before. She grew rather irritable, in between her bouts of daydreaming. Even Percy grew so bold as to comment on it; Alice, for her part, told her straightaway she needed to find a new hobby.

"Take up needlepoint or something, for heaven's sake," she said. "You're irritating Mother more than ever with your mooning, and since you never hear her when she yells at you, she's taken to yelling at me instead."

But Nellie didn't take up needlepoint. She was perfectly content to let her mind settle ever more deeply into the prospect of the future – and run to the window twice a day to see whether the post was being delivered yet. Keeping quiet about her prospects grew ever more difficult; she could not even trust Alice with the secret, as her sister was unpredictable enough that she might decide to share this valuable piece of information with their mother before it was the proper time. It was only Cousin Lacey she could speak to, and then only in her letters, which was certainly not as much of an outlet for her feelings as a conversation in person would have been. If only her father would let her go to Philadelphia. But then, if he had, she might never have felt the need to apply at the agency to begin with, and Blake Irons, her husband-to-be, would remain yet in her imagination.

Some days, she felt as though he were a figment of her imagination, still. Then she would have to get his letter out again and read over it once more, tracing the firm black lines of his steady penmanship, oddly legible for a man's handwriting, reassuring herself that it wasn't something she had simply made up out of a surfeit of daydreaming. No, it was real. And someday soon, she would receive his reply…

And finally, at long last, someday came.

She was seated at her vanity, debating over which earrings she should wear when first she met Blake, when she heard the familiar creak of the garden gate. It was eleven o'clock, far too early in the day for her father to arrive home for luncheon, and they weren't expecting anyone until their engagements that evening. The post, however, had not yet been delivered. She bolted up from her chair and to the window, just in time to see the top of the boy's hat go past beneath.

Today was the day. She knew it, in her heart, and the thought that her mother might open Blake's letter and find out the plan before she was ready to tell it lent haste to her feet. She sped down the stairs and made it to the door before the postboy knocked. Opening it, she slipped outside and closed it behind her.

"Ah, there you are," she said, breathless. "I was just – going out for a walk. What good timing you have."

Somewhat bemused, the young man handed over the letters for the Williams household and left again, ushered away by the pointed, "Thank you, goodbye," Nellie gave him. She slipped back into the house, her heart pounding. Her mother came around the corner just as she put the envelope with her name on it into her pocket.

"Nell?" Adelaide Williams gave her older daughter a slightly suspicious frown, which was met with an effusive smile and what was practically a leap forward toward the stairs.

"Letters for you, Mother." She pushed them into her mother's hands and then headed back to her room at top speed. "I'm sure they're important, you'd better read them at once."

"Goodness, Eleanor, what a strange young woman you are. I can't think where you get it from," she heard her mother muttering behind her. But now she was back in her room, with the door closed behind her, alone at last – alone with Blake's letter.

Fingers trembling, she opened it.

. . .

My dear Miss – Williams.

I'm so pleased to put a name to the unknown – and I'll be even more pleased to put a face to it as well.

Thank you for your letter. Thank you first for your patience and understanding with me – I'm glad to know my words were not too loony for your taste, though I have to say I'm a little doubtful that they were as "delightfully refreshing" as you state, because I know myself a little too well. No one has ever said that I'm either of those things, and I reckon I'm a bit too old to start now – but I'm glad to find my silly letter didn't make you think twice about getting married entirely.

Thank you secondly for telling me so much about you. Your way of expressing yourself puts my little missive to shame, but then I suspect women have a naturally more poetic manner of writing than men do. Maybe I'm wrong about that in some instances, but no livery stable owner ever went into fine literature as a career, as far as I know, so it's certainly true in my case. Regardless, with your letter I can all the more clearly imagine what our life will be like. I've slept with it under my pillow since it arrived, and my dreams have been all the sweeter for it, I'm sure.

You speak of daydreams – well, I'm a little abashed, as I'm a grown man and likely you'll think I shouldn't spend time woolgathering. But the truth is, there's quiet times in my line of work, and though I try to spend them reading or doing something educational, I admit that my imagination sometimes gets the better of me. Here is my daydream: I walk beside the creek that runs through Fort

Regent, turning the mill and keeping our trees green and verdant. Beside me, the love of my life – you. In front of me, the sun is beginning to set. We walk together into the gilded light.

Now I'm all embarrassed, but I'm going to send you this letter anyhow because it's the eighth time I've tried to write it, and no matter how I try, it never seems to come out quite right. Better something than nothing. Besides, the most important part is to ask you to come west to Wyoming and marry me as soon as you're able. Maybe that seems awful sudden – well, maybe it is. I guess that's how the matrimonial agency works, though, and in truth I feel I know enough about you to be ready to ask you. What I don't know about you, I look forward to finding out.

Waiting bareheaded in the summer rain for your reply.

Yours,

Blake Irons

PS. It really is raining here right now. The skies just opened up and let it out, but it's a soft rain all the same, and warm. The light is silver, and I can hear thunder in the distance. There's adventure on the horizon.

If she had written the letter herself, Nellie thought, it could not have been a more perfect complement to her daydreams. She put it down in her lap, running her fingertips over it, smoothing it reverentially, and then looked up and out the window. It seemed there were rainclouds gathering here, too, and she imagined they were the same ones that had released the summer storm in Wyoming, following Blake's letter to give the same silvery light to its recipient.

There was no question about her reply to his proposal – as quickly as this had all happened, her heart was involved, and deeply so. Her desire for love and adventure was being fulfilled, and in the most wonderful way possible. She would write to him tonight and pack her things and hop on a train west the very next morning.

Oh, she knew her parents were bound to be doubtful, frustrated, mistrustful, even angry.

But she didn't care. They would get past that as soon as they understood how happy she was – how happy she was going to be.

She would face up to anything, even the wrath of her father, for the sake of the man who had written her this letter.

She would face up to anything – anything – to follow her dreams, wherever they may lead.

CHAPTER 6

Of course, nothing went as smoothly as Nellie had hoped. Yes, her parents caused a fuss, with her mother in particular practically fainting onto the sofa – an overly-dramatic reaction to the news that their older daughter was engaged to a respectable livery stable owner, in Nellie's opinion. And her father declared any discussion was pointless, as he would refuse to budge on his refusal to withhold his blessing. Nellie pointed out that she did not require his blessing, and the argument only escalated from there.

Alice took her older sister's side, which was a surprise given the circumstances, but it did not help matters when she said, vehemently, "Suppose this is her only chance to get married." Nellie took some offense at the implication, and it immediately reminded both of their parents of the question of Percival Owens.

"I have not agreed to an engagement with anyone else," Nellie said hotly, "and if Percy Owens thinks I'm obliged to him, then he has another thing coming."

She did feel somewhat remorseful over the matter later when she thought of it. Percy had been kind to her, and his main fault was simply that she did not love him. And that wasn't really his fault at all, was it? At any rate, by the time her father demanded, the following morning, that she tell Percy in person she had no intention of marrying him, she was willing to do so. She did not owe him her hand in marriage, but perhaps she did owe him an explanation.

The interview itself was short – Percy took the news like a man, she thought warmly, though she was mostly just glad to have it over and done with – but it required that she spend another two days at home before she could get on the train. And then the tickets were difficult to procure, as it seemed everyone was inexplicably heading west for the autumn. Perhaps, she thought, they all had the same desire for adventure she felt herself; but it seemed unlikely.

All in all, it was nearly a solid week after she had received Blake's letter of proposal that she finally gave her family a final embrace, said goodbye to her old life, and climbed aboard the train.

She would miss her parents, and especially Alice – her emotions weren't entirely wrapped up solely in the thought of her life to come. But her love for them paled next to the excitement of the great adventure that now stretched in front of her. When the train began to judder into motion, she squeezed her eyes tightly shut for a moment, holding her breath – when she opened them again, she felt almost like a different person. Eleanor Williams – soon to be Eleanor Irons – no longer of Middleburg, Virginia, but instead belonging to Fort Regent, Wyoming. The hard-working, iron clad, adventuresome wife of a hard-working, iron clad, adventuresome frontier man. Madame Livery Stable. She could see it now. They would fight off bandit attacks side by side. Perhaps he would run for mayor.

For the first few days of the journey, she was largely sustained by her daydreams. The days passed by with relative smoothness, especially as compared to the tumultuous week before she had left. She was free to watch the landscape slip by and build her new life around herself, brick by brick. She wrote letters to Alice and to Lacey, describing the new things she saw and rhapsodizing over what she imagined the future to be like. There were no bandits, which was something of a pity; but, she reasoned, a girl couldn't have everything.

It wasn't until she reached the beginning of the end – the switch point to the last leg of her trip – that disaster struck.

At first it didn't seem like much of a disaster. It took place in a town named Bear Springs, Nebraska, near the border with Wyoming. She got off the train to change to another, the last portion of the trip, heading directly north. The station was busy, with passengers and conductors and pageboys running back and forth; far more hectic than she would have expected for a town named Bear Springs. She consulted her ticket and found that her train ought to be waiting.

But there was no other train to be seen. Though this platform was clearly designed to be a meeting place for conveyances branching out in different directions, the only train in evidence was the one from which she had so recently disembarked. Frowning in puzzlement, she took a firmer hold on her valise and went to find someone to ask about this new development.

The elderly man behind the ticket counter just shook his head at her.

"You ought to have been told by now," he said admonishingly, as though her lack of information was her own fault. "The tracks are under repair. Ain't no trains running north to Wyoming just now."

"But I bought a ticket all the way through," she protested, digging it out of her pocketbook and brandishing it at him. "Straight through to Fort Regent – it says so right here."

He took the ticket from her, looked at it, then handed it back.

"Sure does."

"But where is the train?"

"I told you," he repeated, with a heavy display of patience. "Ain't no trains running north to Wyoming just now. The tracks weren't safe." He grinned suddenly. "Heck, you ought to be grateful you're not in a train headed north – better to wait it out here in Bear Springs than sitting in the hot sun five miles outside of North Point, Wyoming."

Nellie wasn't at all sure that it was any better. Doing her best to fend off the frustration that leaked around every word, she said, "Well, how long do they expect it to take?"

The ticket master shrugged inelegantly.

"Could be a few days – more likely a few weeks. Train tracks don't just magically mend, it takes real work from real men. Heard they brought in a chain gang all the way from Missouri."

Nellie had no opinion on the idea of the chain gang being imported from such a far-flung place, as opposed to simply using the local convicts. She had lost all desire to converse with the ticket seller, not that she had much of a desire to begin with. With only the empty assurance that the rest of her journey had been postponed for at least a few days, if not a few weeks, she went and sat on a bench at the end of the platform to have a good think about the whole thing.

It really was incredibly frustrating, was what she thought. She lost several moments to unfruitful self-pity before her naturally sunny nature began slowly to reassert itself. It was true, the idea of waiting for weeks on the train was unpalatable. But trains were not the only method of getting from one place to another. There were other possibilities; slower, it was true, and perhaps more uncomfortable, but not entirely reliant on tracks, either.

She could hire a coach.

The idea flashed into her mind like lightning. The more she thought about it, the more she liked it. Yes, she could hire a coach – that was a suitably adventurous way to continue her journey, wasn't it? She could picture it now, her slightly delayed arrival in Fort Regent, met by an adoring and admiring Blake Irons. *The train wasn't running? However, did you manage to get here after all? How clever you are, my dear Miss Nell – I mean – may I call you my dear Miss Nell? We'll be married in half an hour, after all...*

But how did one go about hiring a coach? And, she thought with a guilty start, had she the money for it? She'd brought her own savings, as well as a bit of the money from the petty cash drawer at home, which was usually set aside for household items. She had convinced herself that taking it was a reasonable precaution, and that it was something like a dowry from her parents, and she would return it if at all possible. Surely hiring a coach to travel all the way to Fort Regent would put paid to that, though.

She was still thinking deeply over her options, seated on the bench, and watching her former fellow passengers when she noted the obvious distress of one young woman, who was also enduring her turn at speaking with the ticket seller. From the gesticulations of the woman, and the staid, unflappable expression on the face of the ticket seller, Nellie understood that the poor unknown was likely going through much the same frustration that she herself had so recently undergone. As the young woman turned abruptly away from the counter, shaking her head, Nellie found herself on her feet, moving toward her.

"Hello," she said, holding a hand out and smiling warmly. "I see that you too have met our mutual enemy."

The young woman glanced at Nellie's hand, then took in the meaningful gaze that Nellie sent in the direction of the counter. The tightness of her face relaxed somewhat and she half-laughed, shaking Nellie's hand.

"Yes, unfortunately. Goodness, what an infuriating man. I don't like to speak ill of strangers, but..."

"It's better to speak ill of strangers than it is of friends," Nellie pointed out pragmatically. "They're less likely to call you to account for it. But I certainly agree with you. He was no help at all. I suppose you're looking for your train north."

"Yes, I am. He tells me that there's no hope of catching it before at least a few days."

"He told me the same," Nellie sympathized.

The young woman put a hand to her forehead, closing her eyes for a moment as though she was in pain. Now that

Nellie could get a better look at her, up close, she saw that she must be a bit older than Nellie had originally thought. She estimated that there must be at least five years between the two of them, which would put the other woman around twenty-seven. But her face was unlined, fresh, and quite pretty; it was only the frustration in her eyes and her direct manner that showed she was not younger than Nellie.

"I cannot simply wait around for who knows how long," she said. "I must get to Fort Regent as soon as possible, or my position will be given away."

"You were going to Fort Regent?"

"I am going to Fort Regent. Nothing's going to stop me, not a late train, not that – that – ticket seller." The woman gestured back over her shoulder, evidently at a loss for an acceptably polite term for the man who had so recently irked them both. Nellie couldn't help but laugh.

"I am, too," she said. "I've got a husband waiting for me – that is, a groom. That is, I'm engaged to someone there."

"Oh," said the woman, giving her a look of sympathy. "Of course, you must be very eager to get back to him. I can understand how you feel."

"Well, I've never met him yet," Nellie said, blushing a little to say this to a stranger. The slightly quizzical glance she got in return made her blush even harder. "I wrote to a matrimonial agency, you see, and…"

"Oh, one of those," said the other woman, waving a hand dismissively as though she'd come across dozens in her time. "Well, I certainly hope for the best for you, young lady. Just remember there's no guarantee with such a match – no guarantee that you'll love the man, and no guarantee that you'll even like him."

"I'm not worried over that in the least," Nellie assured her, not taking offense. "We've exchanged letters, and I believe we'll fall in love at first sight."

"I do hope so, for your sake," said the woman, but she remained obviously doubtful. Nellie decided to set this aside for the moment in favor of a more pressing matter: the hiring of a coach.

"I had an idea," she said. "Since we cannot take the train, suppose we look for another avenue? Suppose we hire a stagecoach? It would be ideal," she added swiftly, in case the woman was thinking of objecting, "if we could share it. Especially since we are both so eager to get to Fort Regent and don't want to wait. What do you think?"

The woman put a hand to her chin, eyeing Nellie with a thoughtful gaze that seemed to size her up completely.

"It's not a bad idea," she said at last. "I'd venture to say it's a very good one."

She glanced to the side, and Nellie followed her gaze to see a small pile of suitcases. On top of them sat a small boy, four or five years old, watching them with wide eyes.

"It isn't just me – it's my boy, too. Billy. If it was me alone, I might simply wait it out – but it isn't. I've secured a position at the general store in Fort Regent, through a friend, and if I'm not on time to take my place behind the counter, I'm afraid they'll give it to the next interested party. I cannot lose another job – I have two mouths to feed."

Nellie nodded eagerly.

"I understand completely," she said. "Responsibility is a heavy thing to wear on your shoulders – how soon do you suppose a coach could get us to Fort Regent?"

"From here?" the woman said thoughtfully. "It would take at least three days, if we drove straight through. More, if the road is bad or the horses are slow. But it's certainly a better prospect than waiting for the train."

Nellie smiled and stuck out her hand once more for a shake to seal the bargain.

"My name is Nellie Williams," she said, and corrected herself. "Eleanor, that is."

"Eleanor?" said the woman, raising an eyebrow.

Nellie laughed, self-consciously.

"I'd intended to try it out," she said. "I was born Eleanor, of course, and I thought for my new life, perhaps it would suit me best. But when I say it, all I hear is my mother shouting up the stairs."

The other woman laughed, too, and her laugh was warm and understanding.

"I'm Susan Platt," she said. "Susan – not Sue, unfortunately. I always wanted to be a Sue, but it just didn't suit me." She smiled. "Much like Eleanor doesn't suit you. You're Nellie, through and through. And I'm sure your husband, once you get to Fort Regent and meet him, will be delighted you made it after all."

"Thank you – I certainly hope so."

"Have faith," said Susan Platt, though she still looked as though she herself weren't entirely convinced. She turned toward the pile of suitcases and little Billy, gesturing to him to come their direction. "I have a feeling there's a rough road ahead, but no doubt if we pull together, we can make it through with flying colors."

"Yes," Nellie said, watching the train begin to puff back out of the station, on its way. "The greatest part of the adventure is ahead – I just know it."

CHAPTER 7

On Monday afternoon, Blake Irons took care to look spiffy. He dusted off his best jacket and unrolled the sleeves on his shirt. He put on suspenders. He gathered a bouquet of wildflowers. He even played with the idea of adding his grandfather's bowtie, but he was stopped short by his realization that it might be a bit too much. On top of that, he wasn't sure how to tie it.

After a final inspection in the mirror, he stepped out into the streets of Fort Regent and walked the three blocks to the small train station.

There, he waited.

…and waited.

The wildflowers were wilting in his hand. Frowning in puzzlement, he went in search of Charley Holloway, who usually sold the tickets and was not at his post. He tracked him down at last in the saloon.

"Charley."

"Hello, Blake." the young man greeted him cheerfully, and took a swig of his ale. "What are you doing here? It ain't Saturday."

"No, it's Monday – Monday, Charley. What happened to the train?"

"Oh." Charley waved a hand dismissively. "I got the wire this morning. The tracks were broken just south of North Point. No train running today."

Blake slumped into the chair across from him, frowning more deeply.

"No train today," he repeated, unable to keep the disappointment from his voice. He had been so vividly, so enthusiastically, looking forward to this day, to meeting Nellie Williams. "But – tomorrow, Charley? Tomorrow, it'll be here?"

Charley shrugged, paying more attention to his ale than he was to his friend.

"Dunno," he said. "No one does. Tracks are tricky things, and chain gangs are even trickier. Could be a few days. Could be a week. Could be more."

He seemed to register at last that Blake was staring at him, aghast, and blinked curiously at him.

"What's the problem?"

Blake opened his mouth to answer, then shut it again. It was no use pouring out his worry or distress to Charley – he had yet to tell anyone in Fort Regent he was engaged to be married. He'd wanted to wait until Nellie arrived so he could announce it with her standing there by him, arm in arm – he had a feeling that she would appreciate it as a romantic gesture.

Instead of answering, he said, "Where did they stop it, Charley? If it's south of North Point..."

"Oh, um..." Charley frowned thoughtfully. "Bear Springs, Iowa, if I recall correctly. That's the next large town down, and the train is stopped just outside it."

"The Eastern line runs through there, too, doesn't it?"

"Yep," Charley said, reaching for his ale again. "But that one keeps heading west-east."

"Yes, I know..." Blake lapsed into thought. Nellie had been on the Eastern line; she would have had to change at Bear Springs to head north to Wyoming. Why, she still must be there in Nebraska. She would have arrived that very morning.

The decision was made practically before he even gave it any thought. He stood up from the table so quickly that Charley's ale glass wobbled, and he had to grab for it to keep it from going over.

"Thanks, Charley."

"Sure enough. Say, what's the matter, Blake? You sure are acting funny. You look mighty spruced up, too."

"Nothing," Blake told him. "Nothing at all." Then he eyed his friend closely. "Say, you'll be out of a job for a few days while you wait for them to repair the line, won't you?"

"I will, at that," Charley agreed frankly. "I've had to promise Nathan I'm good for credit in order to get any ale."

"What do you think about coming to work for me for a little while? Just to keep an eye on the place, feed the horses."

"Well, I…" Charley narrowed his eyes at Blake. "Wait, why can't you do it?"

"I've got somewhere to go."

"Where are you going? What are you doing?"

Blake grinned down at his friend.

"I've got a package to collect," he said. "In Bear Springs."

CHAPTER 8

Susan had speculated about the slowness of the horses. However, she had said nothing about the slowness of the driver.

Within the first hour of hiring the coach, boarding, and beginning their journey, Nellie had a sinking feeling this wasn't quite as good of an idea as she had initially thought. Yes, it would get them there eventually – but how long it would take was impossible to speculate.

For that matter, there was also the question of whether they would still be in one piece by the time they arrived.

The second time that she nearly bounced right off the bench seat and onto the floor, she pushed herself against the back of the seat, propping herself up against the floor with her legs tensed and rigid.

"I've never been in a stagecoach before," she confessed to Susan. "Is it always like this?"

Susan shook her head.

"Not always," she managed in between jouncing. "It certainly isn't as smooth as traveling by train – but I think there might be something wrong with the wheel."

It was amazing, Nellie reflected, how they could be simultaneously seeming to carom off each and every rut in the road at once while also moving with such turtle-like slowness. They had only undergone a small percentage of the trip; an overwhelming majority remained, and already she had a headache. Would they make it?

Was this the true meaning of adventure – discomfort and a headache? She was beginning to regret, just a little bit, her idea of hiring the coach at all. But at least they were moving forward, instead of simply sitting and waiting back in Bear Springs, Iowa. A place which she had no desire to ever return to.

Susan, she was sure, felt much the same way.

In the short time since they had sprung their idea and tracked down a coach driver – with the dubious assistance of the ticket seller, who seemed pleased to have them out of his sparse hair but remarkably unreliable as to any of his guidance and advice – Susan had proven to be a steady, thoughtful woman with a deliberate manner and a determination that matched Nellie's own. She didn't seem to have the recurrent bouts of daydreaming, however; no, it was clear that her feet were solidly on the ground. Her intentions were to provide for her son in the best way she knew how, and that meant arriving in Fort Regent to take up her new employment. Nothing was going to stand in her way, as she had even expressed vocally to Nellie not a minute after they had first met.

As to Susan's past, and the mystery of where her husband might be, Nellie shied away from asking just yet. She was happy enough to share her own story, simple as it might be, but she had a feeling Susan's past was not as easily told – or as painless. She wore a simple golden band on her wedding ring finger, it was true, but with Susan's determination and commitment to her goals, Nellie wouldn't have been surprised to find that it was simply to ward off any questions regarding her marriage – or any approach from other interested gentlemen.

Billy was quiet, peacefully sitting next to his mother and playing with a stuffed bunny that had been expertly made from an old towel.

A particularly hard jolt knocked Nellie out of her thoughtful reverie. Across the coach from her, Susan gave a wince and pressed a hand to her forehead.

"Headache?" Nellie asked her sympathetically. "I've got one myself, now. This road is awful."

"I wish he would go a bit faster," Susan said, without directly answering the question. "It's been two hours now, and I can still see the outskirts of Bear Springs. It's almost as though we're traveling backwards."

"We aren't, are we?" Nellie bolted forward and looked out the window.

Despite herself, Susan gave a chuckle at her younger friend's reaction.

"No," she said, "not really. It just feels that way. We'll get there, never you fear."

"Perhaps it would have been faster to wait for the train," Nellie grumbled, sinking back into her seat, which jostled her so hard at that very moment it nearly catapulted her across the coach. "Goodness. I never thought coach travel would be quite like this."

"It startles me to know you've never been in a coach."

"Well, I've been in a hansom cab – but I know that isn't exactly the same thing. We have cobbled streets in our town, for one thing." She shook her head. "I've never really gone anywhere, and so I've never had call to get into a stagecoach before. I don't reckon I'll ever want to again, at this rate."

"Think of it as a learning experience," Susan suggested. "After all, you're going to marry a man who lives in Wyoming, practically in the middle of nowhere – at least, compared to where you're from."

"Middleburg isn't such a big town."

"The size of it doesn't matter. It has cobbled streets, you said so yourself. It's civilized."

"You're right," Nellie said, pondering over this and realizing the benefit of the journey upon which she had so rashly embarked. "This is a good experience for me – why, you've got to be tough to marry a man who runs a livery stable, don't you?"

Susan looked as though it was a great effort to control her laughter – but she was succeeding, simply by dint of being so very determined by nature.

"Yes," she said gravely. "Very tough."

"Then this is good for me," said Nellie decisively. "I'll be tough in no time."

"Indeed," agreed Susan, as the coach gave another jounce. "Although a cook would argue that all of this should have a tenderizing effect…"

Another bounce, another jolt, and suddenly there came a cry from the driver and the coach came to a halt. Nellie leaned forward once more and poked her head out the window.

"Is something wrong?"

The driver was a kindly old fellow. When she'd first laid eyes on him, she had worried he might not make it through a three-day trip to Fort Regent. Now that she had experienced his driving style first-hand, she thought perhaps he was more resilient than she had given him credit for. As she watched, he climbed down from the driver's box. She could practically hear his joints creaking.

"Oh, nothing, nothing, young miss – only the horse needs a bit of a rest."

"The horse?" said Nellie, biting off the sentence before it could finish, …or you?

"He's an old fella," said the driver blithely, apparently unaware of the irony of this statement. "He'll take a bit more time than some other horses – but then, you said you didn't mind so much about that, provided we could leave right away."

He eyed her, and she had to admit his statement was true. By the time they had located him, it had been so late in the day and she and Susan were both so frustrated they would have hired just about anybody if they had promised to leave immediately.

"Well – how long of a rest does he need?"

The driver looked at the skies and shook his head.

"Reckon we'd better camp here for the night," he said. "It'll be dark soon. And you ladies wouldn't like riding in the dark. Might get a bit bumpy."

Nellie opened her mouth – and then shut it again, wisely choosing to keep her thoughts to herself. She sat back and met Susan's gaze. The other woman gave her a tired smile.

"All part of the adventure," she said.

Despite her tiredness, her frustration, and her desire to simply skip forward over the next several days so she could be with Blake Irons right this very moment, Nellie couldn't help but smile back.

"Yes," she said. "All part of the adventure."

CHAPTER 9

The road crept on, and so did the coach. The days all seemed to be running together; surely more than three nights had passed now, the initial estimated time that the coach trip would take, according to Susan. Susan offered no more speculation as to how much longer they had to go. She sat quiet with Billy in her lap, watching the clouds go by outside, occasionally putting a hand to her forehead or wincing in unspoken pain.

For the first time in her life, Nellie had as much time on her hands to daydream as she could possibly have wanted. In fact, she began to grow a little tired of it, though she didn't dare admit it out loud – she scarcely dared to admit it to herself. Over and over, she pictured the events that had for so long occupied her mind: the beauty of her wedding day, the birth of her first child, the inevitable moment when the bandits would ride through Fort Regent, and she would be forced to borrow her husband's rifle and ride into battle at his side.

It was all an adventure, but after the seventh or eighth time of imagining how each step would be taken, what everyone would say, how it would look and feel, it began to pall. She could not wait until she had the real thing; and that was the problem. She had to wait.

The only bit of imagination she could reliably go back to over and over was not imagination at all, but memory. It was the memory of the day she'd received Blake's second letter, the one that invited her to come west and asked her to marry him. When it seemed that Susan and Billy were sleeping, she would take his letters from her pocketbook and read over them again and again, until every word was marked indelibly in her mind. And then she would read them once more, mouthing the words to herself. She could close her eyes and picture herself back home again, with the thrill of the unknown – the dear unknown – waiting for her, all undefined, all a surprise.

Each evening at twilight, they stopped to make camp for the night. That first night, Nellie was acutely conscious of her impatience. She wanted nothing more than to ride on through the night – yes, even risking the exaggerated bumps in the road, though how it could possibly be more strenuous than what they experienced during the day she was not sure. But Susan, for all her determination, seemed rather glad for the rest, and so did the horse. And so did the driver, who was named Joseph Cleveland – "No relation," he'd said cheerily upon introducing himself, which had confused Nellie greatly until she remembered reading in the paper that the new president also shared that surname.

The driver was a cheerful old fellow, given to chatting about the weather and his great-granddaughters, and sometimes how the weather affected his great-granddaughters. He mentioned more than once, over the first days of the trip, that he reckoned this was his last run north.

"Time I settled down," he told them, winking from the other side of the campfire. "Might find me a pretty girl to cook and clean for me, too. Reckon I'll come across one in Fort Regent?"

Nellie and Susan glanced at each other, trying to hide their smiles. He really was a harmless old man, but like most men – especially older ones – he didn't hesitate to flirt.

"Reckon you won't," Nellie told him. "Why, you might have to do what my husband-to-be did, and write for a girl from back east."

She told her story more than once, too; not because she forgot that she had told it, but because he forgot that he had heard it. He would lie on his bedroll on the far side of the fire, a hand on his chest as though he was trying to keep his heart still and ask them to tell him about themselves. Susan did not venture much more about her past than Nellie had already discovered. She left it up to Nellie to share what she liked.

All in all, though it was a much longer journey than she had expected it to be—it was a relatively pleasant one, now that she was growing adjusted to the roughness of the roads. It couldn't be that much longer, she told herself every morning – and again every evening, as they spread out their blankets once more.

It was all part of the adventure – and what an adventure it was turning out to be.

It was on the morning of the fifth day that something seemed to go wrong.

They didn't notice it at first. Susan seemed slightly livelier than she had been from the beginning of the trip, and Nellie was determined to take advantage of this and try to get to know her new friend a bit better. Her eyes were bright, almost startlingly so, and she bounced Billy on her knee, though it was a wasted effort as the road was doing that quite well on its own.

They chatted along as the day began to wind into afternoon, and neither of them noticed they had taken a slight turn. The turn gradually grew more pronounced, and by the time the coach began to slow, Nellie realized the sun had shifted position to shine directly into her eyes, whereas it had been behind them since they'd left. Of course, the sun could not have shifted so – rather, they must have shifted. She was on the verge of calling out to Joe Cleveland and asking him whether he was taking a detour or a shortcut when the coach, which had already been slowing, suddenly stopped completely.

Nellie and Susan stared at each other.

There came a soft whicker from the horse, and what seemed like an answering moan, scarcely audible, from Joe.

"Joe? Joe."

Nellie was out of the coach before she even realized she had moved. Racing around to the front, she stopped, aghast at the sight that met her. The horse had his head up, giving her an inquisitive sound as she came up. The driver was slumped to the side on the bench seat of the driver's box. The reins had dropped from his hands.

"Billy, stay in the coach," Susan ordered her son, coming up behind Nellie. She put a hand on her shoulder. "Let me get to him."

A hand to her mouth, Nellie stepped back, and Susan took her place, climbing up into the box with scarcely a second of hesitation, her skirts swirling around her. She put a firm hand on each of Joe's shoulders and pulled him upright, but he was dead weight and simply slid back down again as soon as she let him go. Nellie gasped, and Susan pressed the heel of her hand to the man's chest, freezing for a moment. After what seemed to Nellie like a very long time, she shook her head regretfully.

"Nothing to be done for him," she said. "I'm afraid he's dead."

Despite her determination to say strong, Nellie felt tears sting at her eyes. They had only known the old man for such a short time, and yet he had been so pleasant, so cheerful. She felt the slice of guilt over how irritable she had been regarding his slowness. He must have been older even than she realized, to have died like this. Unless there was something else that he'd not known about, some illness, perhaps his heart…

She ventured, "What was it? What could have…"

Susan shook her head again.

"I don't know," she said. "Perhaps he was ill – but perhaps he was simply very old." She stepped back to the edge of the box and looked up a last, taking in their surroundings. "Whatever the case, I'm afraid he has not been guiding the horse for some time now. We're far off the roadway."

Nellie's heart faltered, and she looked around as well, realizing for the first time that their surroundings didn't look much like the path they had been following at all. Behind them, the way they had come, was a stand of dark firs. Ahead of them was clear, but the path wasn't visible from where she stood. She held her breath to listen; from far away came the sound of moving water.

Susan sat down on the edge of the box, facing Nellie. Her face was suddenly pale, and she dabbed at her damp forehead with the back of her hand.

"I'm sorry you had to be the one to find him like that," Nellie said in a small voice, reaching up to her new friend. She took Susan's hand; it was a bit clammy, and strangely cold. Nellie wondered if Susan's headache was getting worse, possibly affecting her stomach as well. She was on the verge of asking but Susan simply squeezed her hand, and then let it go.

"Well," she said, "there's no use crying over spilt milk."

"What do we do?"

Susan shook her head.

"I'm afraid we'll have to bury him. I don't know how much longer it will take to get to Fort Regent."

Nellie swallowed hard, a lump appearing suddenly in her throat, and nodded. She looked around them. The horse had its head down and was beginning to graze, confident that the humans would sort things out. It had found a peaceful area thickly carpeted with grass; at the end of summer, this was a good sign. Perhaps the earth would be damp, and easier to dig into.

"We haven't a shovel," said Susan musingly.

Despite the older woman's obvious ill health, she seemed to be taking all of this quite calmly. Nellie couldn't help but speculate that perhaps this wasn't the first time she had assessed a situation that involved unexpected death; could that, maybe, be the painful secret of her past? This was no time to ask, however much she wanted to. If Susan could be calm and matter-of-fact about all of this, then so could Nellie – if she put her mind to it.

She looked about her, then back at the stand of trees that were not so far away.

"I'll find a branch," she said. "Maybe that will help."

Ten minutes of rooting through the first trees she came to furnished her with a broken branch that featured a flat, slanted portion where it had become separated from the trunk. It was better than nothing, and she took it back to the coach, stripping off the dead needles to make it easier to hold. Susan was in the coach with Billy in her arms. When Nellie glanced inside, she saw that Susan's eyes were closed.

She wanted to ask if she was all right – she wanted to ask whether she would come and help – but she said nothing and went to start to dig on her own.

She had been at it for half an hour when Susan emerged from the coach, slowly, and came to help. She got on her knees beside the hole that Nellie had begun and dug in with both hands.

Between the two of them, it took several hours to scratch out a hole that was anywhere deep enough to put the poor old driver. Moving the stiff body was a difficult experience that, Nellie was afraid, would haunt her dreams forever. At last, the deed was done, and the dirt piled up in what seemed suddenly a tragically small mound. Susan laid a few stones at the head of it, and the two women stood together in the near-dark, quietly. Billy, who had emerged from the coach unseen a while before, came and held his mother's hand.

"Well," said Susan at last, "we did say that it was an adventure ahead of us…"

"Yes," said Nellie. "I suppose we did. About the only thing that hasn't happened so far is being attacked by outlaws."

As time went on, she had to admit, she was enjoying the adventure less and less. But she tried to pick up her spirits; after all, she had wanted to become tougher, hadn't she? She wanted to be worthy of being the wife of a midwestern man, able to handle anything life threw at her. She just hadn't expected life would throw something like burying someone in the middle of the woods.

She took a deep breath, fending off tears of exhaustion, and looked around them.

"It's too dark to try and find the pathway now," she said. "We'd better make camp here, don't you think?"

Susan gave her an appraising look. "I think you're right," she said.

Nellie nodded, wiping her dirty hands together slowly, wondering if she could ever get the earth from under her fingernails.

"Tomorrow morning," she said, "we'll find the way forward – and we'll get to Fort Regent."

She knew that this hope – the hope of reaching Blake Irons at last, being clasped in his arms and reassured that everything would be all right – was the only thing that would get her through the night.

CHAPTER 10

By the second hour of the next morning's journey, Nellie was worried that her optimism had been sadly unfounded.

The pathway seemed to elude them, no matter how hard they searched. It baffled her, how they could have gotten so badly lost in such a short time. Were they wandering in circles? She was terrified they were, terrified they would never reach the roadway, let alone Fort Regent – terrified the three of them would die out there in the vast wilderness of Wyoming, with no one even to bury them like poor Joe Cleveland…

And Susan's condition wasn't helping her to feel any better.

The two of them were taking turns on the driver's cart. But when Susan started out that morning, it was only a matter of just a little while before the horse began dragging its steps, moving more and more slowly. Nellie poked her head out to try and see what was happening, what might be holding them up, but there was no reason she could find.

"Susan?"

There was a pause, and then a faint, "Yes?"

"Susan," Nellie said firmly, fear darting into her heart, "stop the coach for a moment."

There was no doubt about it: Susan was very ill. Her face was paler than ever, her hands freezing cold, her forehead burning up. Her eyes were half-closed, and when Nellie tried to take the reins from her, she shook her head with a grimace.

"No – I'll be fine…"

"You're not fine," Nellie told her sternly. "You must get down and get into the coach with Billy."

"No…"

"Susan…Billy needs you." She didn't know what else to say. The woman was stubborn in her reliance on her own strength, and Nellie had a feeling that nothing else but an appeal to her motherly instincts would convince her to take care of her own health. She held her breath; to her relief, the gambit worked.

Susan shifted slowly, and Nellie had to help her down the stairs, but a matter of moments saw her safely stowed back in the coach, with little Billy at her side. The boy turned to Nellie with wide eyes, clearly frightened, and she put a hand on his shoulder, trying to comfort him. But there was nothing she could say, no assurance she could make, that she knew to be true. Susan was very ill – and she didn't know what was going to happen.

Suppose Joe had died of some sort of illness, rather than his heart? Suppose Susan had that same illness? Suppose…

But she couldn't think of it. She couldn't even let herself entertain for a moment that Susan might also fall to the viciousness of death.

She just had to keep going – and she had to do it alone.

Wearily, she climbed back up into the driver's box and took up the reins.

Given that she'd never so much as been inside a stagecoach just a few short days before, it was almost shocking to realize how much had changed between now and then. Here she was, not only on a coach but actively driving the horse; the horse, luckily, was a calm and patient animal, easy to direct and not given to rebellion. Learning how to give guidance had certainly been a process, but she felt they had worked it out between them.

It was past noon now, the sun beating down overhead. It wasn't nearly as hot here as it got in Middleburg, but it certainly wasn't cool and refreshing either. She knew the food they had brought with them for the journey, limited enough even at the beginning, was dangerously low. The water in the barrel at the back of the coach, too, was nearly gone. They would have to find something to keep them going – or they risked dying of thirst.

She thought hard over her options, looking out at the wide swath of meadow ahead of them. The horse had been moving very slowly, though there seemed to be an old road they were following, half hidden underneath the grass. Perhaps it led to a settlement – or had done, once upon a time. The sound of running water was a bit clearer now. They must have been running parallel to the river.

She took the reins firmly in hand and directed the horse to the right, toward the sound of water. If nothing else, they could refill the water barrel. Cool water might soothe Susan's burning fever, too. And maybe Nellie could catch a fish to eat…

For just the briefest of moments, she could picture it. She caught it with her bare hands, moving more quickly than the eye could see. She brought the quicksilver creature back to the fire that was burning merrily near the coach, with Susan sitting up near it, clear-eyed and on the mend. Billy clapped his hands as Nellie spitted the fish expertly and suspended it over the fire to roast…

But the daydream was gone just as quickly as it had come. It was a forlorn hope. She had no idea how to catch a fish, let alone spit it – and her efforts at building a fire the night before had gone poorly.

Besides all that, she sadly acknowledged that daydreams had simply lost their luster. She didn't need to dream about adventures at all – she was on one.

CHAPTER 11

The journey to Bear Springs was accomplished in far shorter a time than it usually would have taken, thanks to the fact that Blake had borrowed – without permission, which he would have to explain when he returned – the fastest horse that was being boarded in the livery stable.

Even so, it took longer than he wanted it to. Suppose Nellie was just waiting for him? It had been almost a week now since she would have gotten off the train. Surely, she would have gone to an inn or something of the sort – that was only practical. Still, in his mind, he could picture her returning to the empty train station every morning, and only leaving in the evening, waiting for him faithfully, believing that someday he would find her…

The long journey was difficult enough, but it was when he came up against the ticket seller at the train station in Bear Springs that things began to be – irksome.

To start with, the old man claimed he couldn't remember anyone who might possibly have been Eleanor Williams.

"She has dark brown hair," Blake told him. "And gray eyes. Slightly taller than average for a girl from Virginia." He had Nellie's letter with him to remind him of her self-description, but he didn't need to look at it. He had practically committed it to memory.

"Sure," said the ticket seller, arms folded. "But what does she *look* like?"

This was not the first time that he had asked. Blake shook his head, baffled.

"I don't know," he said. "I've never seen her."

"Then how do you know about all of that?"

He brandished the letter.

"Because she told me."

"What some girl writes to you is no concern of mine," said the ticket seller, contriving to indicate that he disapproved greatly of Blake's apparently lax morals. "You can see there's no one waitin' for you here. No one has been waitin' either."

There seemed nothing for it – he was going to get no information at all from the ticket seller. Shaking his head, Blake prepared to turn away.

As a last-ditch effort, he said, trying to find a new avenue, "Suppose that someone wanted to head north from here…"

"I already told you, son. There ain't no trains running now, the tracks are down."

"I know, I know. But if they needed to go north, what would you tell them to do?"

The ticket seller looked thoughtful for a moment.

"Well, I reckon I'd tell them to hire a coach driver and go up that way," he said. "Just like those two young women did the other day."

Blake stood up a little straighter.

"What two young women?"

The old man made a dismissive gesture, waving a hand. "Bah – they didn't know what they were talking about, kept insisting they were getting on the train even though I told them that it wasn't running. I finally got through to them. Next thing I know they're pestering me about where to hire a driver, so I sent them to old Joe Cleveland at the Seven Days Inn." He shook his head. "Don't they know I've got tickets to sell? I can't be standing around explaining things all day to silly girls."

"Joe Cleveland at the Seven Days Inn," Blake repeated. "Thank you, sir."

He bolted for his horse, leaving the old fellow hollering after him.

"It's no use trying to hire Joe – this was his last run."

So Nellie had hired a coach to take her the rest of the way. Her industrious spirit, her ability to find a way around a difficult situation, only reaffirmed Blake's gut feeling that his wife-to-be was an intelligent, spirited woman. It made him smile to picture her setting out on the coach. It made his heart soar to realize she might be waiting for him in Fort Regent even now –

And then his heart plummeted back into place abruptly. He had passed no coach on the way south to Bear Springs. Riders on horseback, yes, but certainly no young women doing so, and not a single coach at all. Was it possible they had found another road? No, if they hired a driver who knew what he was doing, he would know there was really only one fastest route north. Had they taken a wrong turn somewhere and gotten lost?

Anxiety and doubt suddenly assailed him, and he spurred his horse onward toward the Seven Days Inn. The next step was to inquire about this Joe Cleveland and see what he might have done, where he might have gone, other than directly north. Blake hoped the fellow was in his right mind – if the ticket seller was calling him "old" then it gave cause to worry. But there was nothing else to be done at the moment – just seek out information and then, with hope in his heart and a prayer on his lips, go looking for his missing bride.

CHAPTER 12

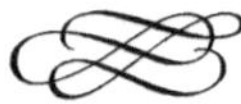

The sound of running water stirred Nellie from her slumber. She opened her eyes and blinked at the skies above her – they were unclouded and a pale, almost translucent blue that could mean either the very early morning or the very early evening. What was she doing outside? She felt a cooling breeze wash over her and sighed, stretching in the grass. Her whole body ached – what had she been doing?

Then she heard a faint sniffle from Billy, and the past few days came rushing back on her all at once.

She'd made it to the running water the night before. It had taken far longer than she'd thought it would; the terrain seemed simple, but it was deceptive, and the cart wheels had gotten stuck in more than one ancient rut along the way. The horse was tired and thirsty, plodding along at a pace that became gradually slower and slower with each passing moment. Finding the river at last had brought a rise to her spirits, even if only temporarily; she'd helped Susan out of the coach and to the water's edge, and Billy had taken off his shoes and rolled up his pant legs and gone wading. She'd been unsure of how to unhitch the horse – and knew she would never get it hitched again if she did – so she led the poor thing as near the water as she could and let it drink, hoping the coach wouldn't simply roll in and get stuck in the mud.

They had slept soon after that, all three of them huddled in the coach. In the night, there had been the sounds of animals, and nervous whickers from the horse.

Now here she was, asleep on the grass of the riverbank. She sat up. Her head was aching, and she was terribly thirsty. Hungry, too. Susan and Billy were still in the coach; she alone must have crept out during the night. She concentrated, but it was an effort – yes, she had come out to check on the horse, unsure of what she could do to protect it but doing her best to soothe its fears. She must have curled up on the grass afterward and fallen back to sleep…

Now that she was seated, she could see the sun was setting, not rising. They had slept through the entire day. Perhaps it wasn't surprising, she thought, considering the exhausting events of the past few days. Still, it made her feel anxious. There was no point in continuing on today – they might as well stay put. In the morning, she could refill the water barrel and they could – well, they could keep going and try to find the road…

The enormity of the task in front of her struck her like a lead weight, and she took a deep breath. To keep Susan and Billy fed and well, to keep the horse fed and watered, to find the road, to get to Fort Regent, to find Blake, who surely must be worried about her and wondering what had happened…

Could she really do it all? How could she be capable of such things when she felt so utterly helpless?

For the first time, Nellie began to wonder whether she had made a mistake.

Perhaps this grand adventure wasn't what she needed – perhaps it wasn't even what she wanted. Perhaps she didn't really want excitement and danger. Out here in the real wild west, trains broke down, people went hungry and thirsty, wild animals roamed. People died and were buried without even a gravestone to mark their passing.

She closed her eyes, fighting the onset of tears. With trembling fingers, she fumbled in her pocket until she found the second letter from Blake.

…I admit that my imagination sometimes gets the better of me. Here is my daydream: I walk beside the creek that runs through Fort Regent, turning the mill and keeping our trees green and verdant. Beside me, the love of my life – you. In front of me, the sun is beginning to set. We walk together into the gilded light…

She had read it over so many times she knew it by heart. Still, she needed to see the words. The ink had blurred from the touch of her fingertips, the paper was crumpled and torn from the wildness of the journey in the last few days, but the feelings that the letter evoked were stronger than ever. Blake Irons was part of her strength. Hope and faith and something to look forward to.

The rest of her strength must come from within.

She pushed herself up to a stand, surveying the small kingdom of her camp. She stowed the letter safely back in her pocket.

The night was upon her once more. She needed a fire. Susan and Billy needed something to eat – there was precious little food left in their stores, but they could have what there was, and surely there must be berries or something to find around here, this late in the summer and near a river. If she built the fire and then led the horse and coach between the fire and the river, it would be safer for the horse. And safer for them, as well – she was sure she'd heard wolves howling in the distance last night.

Well, she had a plan. Now all she needed was to take action.

Shaking off the insidious touch of her own feelings of helplessness, she bit her lip and moved forward.

CHAPTER 13

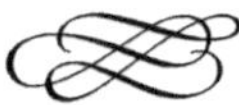

It was growing dark, and Blake's heart was discouraged.

His horse was near exhaustion, and he knew he would have to stop soon. It had been far too long of a day, and tomorrow stretched out ahead of him in much the same fashion. His eyes ached, and he rubbed at them with one hand. Hours upon hours of carefully scrutinizing the roadway as he cantered past as quickly as he dared, looking for any telltale signs where the hired coach might have diverted from the path. So far there had been nothing but a few false alarms, breaks in the vegetation that quickly led to nothing. He was only four hours or so from Fort Regent now, and he was confident he had not yet seen where the coach would have turned.

But that didn't settle his mind any. Nellie was still out there, without anyone to protect her except a driver so aged that the owner of the Seven Days Inn had shaken his head and said, soberly, "I've told him more than once, if he doesn't stop driving and settle down, he's going to die in the driver's box."

Something must have gone wrong, Blake knew it. Even an old and doddery driver would not have turned off the main road, not if he was headed straight to Fort Regent. Something must have happened, and the uncertainty of not knowing was driving him crazy.

He cast a glance at the horizon. The sun had long since set, and the long twilight of summer was almost over. Off to the right and ahead of him, true darkness was creeping forward, enveloping the stand of firs that started a little off the track. The woods obscured everything on that side as far as he could see. There was a river out there somewhere, he knew; the same river that Regent's Creek fed into. He wondered when he would be able to show the beauty of Regent's Creek to Nellie.

He wondered whether it would ever happen at all.

With this fleeting thought came a redoubling of his determination. Yes, he would find her, and he would bring her home safely. He'd promised himself to her, and he wasn't about to give up just because things were tough.

She was out there somewhere – waiting for him.

But as the night fell over the land like a blanket, his hope and faith began to do battle with the armies of despair.

CHAPTER 14

"Tomorrow," Nellie whispered to herself, "we'll find the roadway again…tomorrow."

Off in the distance, she thought she heard something like a footstep, a branch cracking under the weight of an animal. Her head flew up, and she listened intently for a moment – but there was nothing more.

Once more, she repeated the words to herself.

"Tomorrow, we'll find the roadway…"

It was late. The last time she looked at her pocket watch by the light of the nascent fire, it had been after eleven o'clock. She was exhausted – but she could not sleep, not tonight. Her fears of the last night had returned in full force, and she was afraid that if she let the fire go out, the wolves would come and attack the horse. And then where would they be? Susan was too ill to move, and Billy wouldn't leave her side. What would they do?

If something happened to the horse, Nellie told herself, she would have to leave them in the coach and walk until she found help. That was all there was to it – she needed a plan, just in case, and that was the only plan that had any chance of success.

But if she stayed awake, she could defend the horse. And then tomorrow, they would find the roadway…

She didn't sleep, but she did dream. She dreamed that she was back on the train, that the bandits had returned after leaving them in peace. The bandit leader had come back for her. He received her letter in the mail, he told her, and he had been looking for a wife…

Then they were back home in Middleburg, Virginia, she and Susan and Billy. Lacey was coming for a long-awaited visit. If only she could get in touch with Blake Irons, she was sure he would lend them a horse to go and collect Lacey at the train station – but they'd need a coach, wouldn't they? Lacey always traveled with baggage.

Then they were here, in the woods, in the quiet of the night, and she heard a noise that made her sit bolt upright.

It was the faintest whicker from a horse.

She looked at their own horse. The poor thing was much the worse for wear after the last several days and seemed to have taken the death of its master quite hard, for which she could not blame it. It didn't move, but its ears pricked up, and she knew that it, too, had heard the noise.

Her heart beat double-time in her chest, and she got slowly to her feet.

If there was a horse, there was almost certainly a rider.

If there was a rider, this late at night, in the dark, in the wilderness…

Her own words came back to her with a stench of irony.

"About the only thing that hasn't happened to us yet is outlaws."

Well, she wasn't about to let anyone rob them, or – or – or anything else. She'd made it this far, and she was going to make it all the way. She'd protect Susan and Billy and the horse tonight. And tomorrow, they'd find the roadway.

She reached for the stick she'd been using to stir up the fire, put her back to the horse and coach protectively, and stood at the ready, eyes searching the gloom.

Another noise from the unknown horse alerted her.

"Who's there?" she cried.

He stepped into the light without saying anything.

For a moment she fought the uneasy certainty that she knew him, she knew his face, though she could not recall from where. He was tall, broad-shouldered, dressed in dark clothing. He wore no hat, and his hair was thick and black. His eyes were black, too, strikingly so – and they were warm, practically glowing from within. She'd seen eyes like that before – in her dreams…

"Tell me you're not Nellie Williams," he said. "I won't believe it, but…tell me."

She gaped at the outlaw for a moment, and it seemed her entire world revolved around her with a sickening pace until at last the pieces of the puzzle crashed into place, and she regained control of herself enough to say, incredulously, "…Blake?"

A smile spread over his face, and she felt herself blushing hotly. He was the most handsome man she'd ever seen.

"I've found you at last," he said softly.

She flung herself around the edge of the fire, ending up in his arms, holding tightly onto him. Her mother's voice sounded disapprovingly in her head, but she didn't care it was an impropriety to embrace a man whom you had only just this moment met. She felt as though she'd known him forever. He'd inhabited her dreams for so long – how could he be a stranger?

Anyhow, they were engaged to be married.

"I can't believe it."

Her voice was muffled against his shirt front, and he set her back a little and looked down at her, still with that warm smile.

"I believe it," he said.

He cupped her cheek with his hand. Already, though they didn't even know each other, his eyes were full of fondness. There was gratitude there, too, and she thought of his letter. She was the reward to him for being a good man – and he must be her reward, in turn. Her reward for making it through this wilderness.

"There's got to be a story behind all this," he said, looking over at the coach and reaching out to pet the horse's nose.

"Oh, goodness, you have no idea." She put a hand to her forehead. "My friend Susan is in the coach, she's quite ill. I don't know what's wrong, but she's had terrible headaches for days and they've just been getting worse – that's her son Billy looking out the window at us – and the driver, poor old Joe, he passed away and we – well, I'll tell you all about that later. For now, though, Blake…Blake." She clutched at his hand, still scarcely able to believe that he was there, in the flesh. "Blake, you're – you're real, aren't you? I didn't dream you up."

Another grin, and he leaned forward and pressed a kiss to her forehead.

"Does that feel real?"

Nellie gave a tremendous sigh of relief.

"What do we do now?"

"Well," he said, "it's late. So late, it's early – but I reckon you'd rather get on the road back to Fort Regent rather than spend the night out here. If your friend is well enough to ride."

"I think so. We were going to leave again in the morning, though I don't know the way."

"Don't worry, Nell – I know the way."

He tied his horse up to the back of the coach and handed her into the driver's box. He poked his head in at the window for a moment, and she heard him speak in low tones first to Billy and then to Susan, who responded faintly – but at least it was a response. Then he was seated beside her, that reassuring grin in the flickering darkness warming her to her toes, and took up the reins.

"Get along," he said to the horse, and clicked his tongue.

Then they were moving, away from the swiftness of the river, out of the shadowy darkness and into a wide open plain, above which she could see the stars. But they were already fading; the moon was setting, and day was drawing near.

"Well, now," said Blake Irons. "This'll be something to tell our children about."

Nellie laughed. She couldn't help it.

"Only if we want to scare them," she said.

"I thought maybe it'll encourage them to go on big, wild adventures like their mother."

"Do you know, that was all I ever wanted," she said frankly. "When I first wrote to you, that was what I thought I was getting. I thought I was ready for it…until it happened."

He laughed, and her heart sang a little. "I'm afraid Fort Regent isn't going to afford you much excitement and adventure," he said. "It's a peaceful, quiet little town – that's one of my favorite things about it."

Nellie smiled at him. "I never thought I'd say this – but I may have had quite enough adventure for one lifetime," she said. She nudged him with her elbow. "Besides – my husband will be there, so I'm sure I'll be quite content."

He smiled back, his eyes fixed on hers and warm with understanding.

Together, his horse plodding slowly behind them, they drove into the gilded light of the rising sun.

The End

CONTINUE READING...

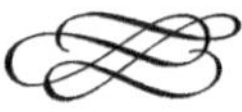

Thank you for reading **Finding Nellie!** Are you wondering **what to read next?** Why not read **The Groom's Secret Kin??** **Here's a peek for you:**

"Mandy! Mandy, wake up."

The voice filtered through her dreams and turned them troubled. The world around her was shaking, trembling violently. The walls were collapsing, the roof about to tumble in. She'd had dreams like this before.

Another strong jostle, and the voice was more insistent now.

"Mandy, *please.*"

Mandy Roseman startled awake to the tear-stained face of her youngest brother, Randall. He sniffled and wiped at his

96

nose with the back of his hand, then flung his arms around her.

"I thought you'd never wake up."

"Shh, shh," she comforted him, sitting up and pulling him into her lap. At only four years old, he was easily the most emotional of the four boys, and particularly prone to bad dreams. "What was it this time?"

"A crocodile." His voice was muffled in her shoulder, but she managed a weary smile.

"A crocodile, was it? Do you know what, Randall?"

"What?"

She set him aside so she could look gravely into his face.

"It's been five hundred years since there was a crocodile sighting in Boston."

Another swipe of his nose with the back of his hand.

"Really?"

She nodded seriously. "Do you think they can hide that long?"

Randall considered this. "No," he said. "They don't even live that long."

Mandy smiled, setting him down at the side of her cot and standing up. She took his hand and began to lead him back to his cot on the other side of the little room. "That's right. Now, maybe there are some old-timer crocodiles out there, but five hundred years? I don't think so, do you?"

"No…"

"So let's get you back to bed, and I'm sure you'll dream of something else this time. What would you like to dream about, Randall?"

His answer was almost immediate.

"Cake."

Visit HERE To Read More!

https://ticahousepublishing.com/mail-order-brides.html

THANKS FOR READING!

If you **love Mail Order Bride Romance, <u>Visit Here</u>**

https://wesrom.subscribemenow.com/

to find out about all **<u>New Susannah Calloway Romance Releases!</u> We will let you know as soon as they become available!**

If you enjoyed *Finding Nellie,* would you kindly take a couple minutes to leave a positive review on Amazon? It only takes a moment, and positive reviews truly make a difference. Thank you so much! I appreciate it!

Turn the page to discover more Mail Order Bride Romances just for you!

ABOUT THE AUTHOR

Susannah has always been intrigued with the Western movement - prairie days, mail-order brides, the gold rush, frontier life! As a writer, she's excited to combine her love of story with her love of all that is Western. Presently, Susannah lives in Wyoming with her hubby and their three amazing children.

www.ticahousepublishing.com
contact@ticahousepublishing.com